NIGHT JOURNEYS

E. C. HIBBS

For Mum, Dad, and Grand

CONTENTS

WALKING WITH STRANGERS

In celebration of

150 years

of

Alice's Adventures in Wonderland

The metronome started to tick.

Once again, Alice began running, forcing herself to not look out of breath already. She turned in every direction she could think of, leaping over giant pencils and hollow dominoes the size of mattresses. In her periphery, she could see the Mouse and the Dodo, both darting aimlessly about like her, but a little slower, so there was less chance of them tripping over their giant padded feet.

"Come on, go faster! We need it faster!"

Alice obeyed, rounding the corner of an oversized book. Suddenly, the Lory came in the opposite direction. Alice yelped, throwing out her hands to cushion the impact, but it still sent her flying backwards into a mushroom. It splintered as she hit it, the papery surface rupturing to expose the wire skeleton underneath.

The metronome instantly shut off.

"Cut! Cut!" Pete shouted.

Alice covered her eyes as she heard the anger in his voice. This was just what she needed.

"Are you alright?" the Lory asked. Its mouth didn't move; the voice came from the actor concealed inside the costume. He slipped a hand through a hidden hole in the animal's wing and held it out for her to take.

"I'm fine," Alice replied as he helped her upright; then called to the director. "I'm so sorry, Pete."

"Of course you are!" he snapped, storming over from the small dais where he'd been standing with the camera. He pointed at the mushroom. "Look at that mess! That's going to take a good two hours to fix!"

"I didn't mean to," Alice insisted. She started to brush the paper mache off her skirt. "It was an accident."

"There's no such things as accidents here," Pete said firmly.

The studio fell into shadow as a heavy cloud drew over, and fat raindrops began to splatter on the roof. The entire building was made from glass, so the sun could bring in enough natural light for the filming to take place, and the outside world soon became distorted as water ran down the panes. Alice shivered under the frilly dress she was wearing.

"Oh, how wonderful," Pete muttered sarcastically; then clapped his hands. "Alright, everyone, we're going to have to stop there for a short while. This weather isn't going anywhere, from the looks of things. Someone help Bill, please!"

The tension relaxed at once. The cameras were carefully covered; the moveable parts of the set dismantled and propped out of the way. A couple of hands sprung forward towards the Lory. Its head was lifted off; the line of hidden hooks and eyes undone from the back. Then it was prised apart, revealing the young man who had been concealed inside.

He breathed deeply, savouring the fresh air, and wandered over to Alice. She rubbed her eyes in exhaustion. The caucus race was one of her favourite parts from the book, but they had been trying to film it all day, and now all she wished was to curl up and go to sleep.

"Wow, it feels good to be out of that thing," Bill smiled. "Are you hurt, dear?"

Alice shook her head. "I suppose I just got a bit agitated. Why can't Pete calm down? What's so important about this scene? The whole point of the race is that there's no order, so why be so fussy about it?"

"Because no matter what we do, it doesn't look *strange* enough."

Alice jumped, whirling around. The director was standing right behind her, inspecting a reel of film from inside one of the cameras. He gave her a long stern look; then strode off to collect his coat and hat.

While his back was turned, Alice stuck out her tongue. "He makes me so edgy when he barks orders like some king. What are we, servants or something?"

"Well, *we* are but players," replied Bill through a chuckle. He got to his feet and motioned towards the door. "Come on, kid, let's go and get some food until this rain blows over."

"I'll be along in a moment," said Alice, motioning at her black strap shoes. "I'd better change into my boots. These will get soaked otherwise!"

Bill nodded; then joined the small crowd leaving the studio. As they stepped outside, Alice faintly caught the aroma of fresh cakes from the bakery across the road. Her stomach grumbled in response, so she hurried behind the set background where she had stored her boots.

Back here, several props and costumes were stowed, creating a labyrinth of creatures, giant playing cards, and too many teapots to count. A stack of doors lay on the floor nearby, each smaller than the one before. They had come from the only scene completed thus far: the Hall of Many Doors, where the adventures into Wonderland began.

At first, Alice had found it amusing that she had the same name as her character. She'd been the right age, with the right blonde hair and the right wide-eyed nature that the production company had been searching for. But creating the first ever movie adaptation of Lewis Carroll's story was a challenge enough without it being directed by the most obnoxious man she'd ever met. Alice had disliked him from the first, so she quickly started calling him the Rat in her head. She supposed it was fitting: he certainly *looked* like a rat.

The White Rabbit costume caught her eye, suspended on its hanger from a metal clothes pole. Its head had drooped over its chest, as though the neck was broken. It was modelled very faithfully after the original illustrations, complete with high-collared jacket, waistcoat, and a golden pocket watch. The watch was a real one, and its ticking sounded abnormally loud. Alice couldn't get it out of her head as she searched among the boxes for her boots.

"I'm sure I left them around here," she muttered; then yawned deeply. The chill of the rainclouds was getting to her. Not even her hunger for the cakes seemed to override it.

The watch carried on ticking.

"Are you tired?"

Alice looked over her shoulder to answer, but there was nobody there. Hadn't she been the last person inside the studio?

"Who said that?" she called. Her voice echoed off the glass.

"I did," said the Rabbit.

Alice's eyes grew wide. She gaped at the limp costume, reaching out gingerly to touch it.

"It's very rude to stare!" the Rabbit snapped suddenly.

Alice leapt back and tumbled into the pile of doors.

"I'm sorry!" she blurted, not sure what else to say.

"So you should be, young lady," the Rabbit mumbled. "Now, I asked if you were tired. Because I speak Tired and Sleeping quite fluently."

It reached up and unhooked its coat from the pole, landing lithely on its feet. The material sagged a little under the weight, but didn't buckle the way Alice expected it to. There was nobody still inside it, was there?

Her cheeks reddened in embarrassment.

"Very funny, Bill," she laughed, picking herself back up. "You got me."

"Silly girl! Bill's the lizard!" replied the Rabbit in a sharp voice. He motioned briskly at his large ears. "Your eyesight must be severely impaired."

"It's not," Alice huffed. She glanced around the side of a giant book to check the studio was actually deserted. Seeing nobody, she turned back to the Rabbit, deciding to hear what it had to say.

"How can you be standing by yourself if there's nobody holding you up?"

"Why ask me?"

Alice hesitated. "Because... you're the only one here to ask."

The Rabbit looked about. "I suppose," he conceded; then reached out and grasped her hand. "Come on. Let's go for a walk."

Alice frowned, but didn't resist, allowing herself to be led through the warren of set pieces. She thought the creature would make an abrupt turn at some point, to avoid hitting one of the walls, but he didn't, and carried on in a straight line.

"Where are we going?" she asked eventually. "The exit's behind us."

"Oh, we certainly can't reach it, then!" declared the Rabbit, straightening his waistcoat in mid-step.

"What? Yes we can, we just turn around."

"Impossible."

"Wait!" Alice wrenched herself free, but couldn't stop her feet from walking. They carried her forwards, keeping perfect pace at the Rabbit's side.

"Wait?" he repeated in an incredulous voice. "There's no such thing as waiting. Nothing waits for nothing, you know."

"No, I don't know," she replied.

"You don't know very much, do you?" said the Rabbit critically.

Alice crossed her arms, not bothering to hide how offended she was. "I know I mustn't go walking with strangers, for one thing. I know Bill, who should be wearing you to make you move about, but he's not here, and no one else is, either. So I don't know who you are, do I?"

"Of course you do. I know you're a girl, so you know I'm a Rabbit."

"No, you're not. You're a costume."

"There! So you do know who I am!"

"That's not a who," Alice argued. "It's a what!"

"Both much of a muchness," the Rabbit said, lazily waving a paw.

Realising she wasn't going to get anywhere with him, Alice decided to stop speaking. At first, she wondered if the Rabbit would realise his insults had gone too far, but upon seeing the conversation was clearly over, he turned his attention to his pocket watch and tutted loudly.

"Two minutes out. It simply won't do!" With that, he smacked it on a tree trunk, never breaking his stride for a moment. "There. That's better."

Alice didn't respond to this either, for she suddenly noticed that the surroundings had changed drastically. It looked as though they were in a huge forest. The paper mache props were still strewn about here and there, and everything was flat, as though it had been painted onto layers of canvas. But the mere fact that they had just walked past a *tree trunk* was enough to tell her they were no longer in the film studio.

"Oh, no," she whispered, holding a hand to her mouth. "I must be dreaming. That's what it was in the book."

"A dream, you say?" The Rabbit looked at her. "Well, if it's a dream, how can anything be a must? The whole point of dreams is that *nothing* must be anything."

Alice shrugged. "I suppose you're right, but if that's the case, how do I know I'll get back? I can't walk through a dream forever. Once everyone's eaten their dinner, I have to be on set again. You as well. We're filming the part when I get stuck in your house next."

"My house?" the Rabbit suddenly cried. "Oh, dear... my poor house!"

"Not now!" Alice insisted, alarmed at his shrill reaction. "I'm sure your house is fine."

"Are you? You know that for certain? But, young lady, we've already established you know nothing!"

Alice was too taken aback to reply, but it wouldn't have mattered either way, for the Rabbit let out a strange whimper and bolted into the trees. Alice quickly gave chase, determined not to lose him.

"Don't go!" she yelled. "Please! I don't know my way!"

"Find it, then!" the Rabbit tossed over his shoulder, before he vanished from sight.

Alice slowed to a halt and clutched at her side, where a stitch had started throbbing. She'd have thought her hours of running the caucus race scene would have meant she could have kept up easily. But, she reminded herself, that was on a set, not in an entire forest.

She looked around her, trying to find a sense of direction. The trees were paper-thin, but layered, like the pictures in a pop-up book. The light seemed to be painted directly onto them, and they loomed out of a shadowed background that was too dark to see beyond five feet. Even the grass was papery, and crumpled as she stepped on it.

"Oh, dear," she muttered. "Well, it's a good thing I came here before I could change my shoes. Boots would cause even more damage!"

"Damage? You don't know anything about damage! You don't eat everything you come across, do you?" a flickering voice wailed from off to the left.

"Who's there?" Alice called. "Where are you?"

"You can't see me? I'm not bright enough for you? Silly girl!"

"Everyone's just as rude as in the book!" Alice said to herself. "Well, at least I don't have to hear it all when we're filming. I'll quiver on the day when movies can actually record sounds as well as images!"

She started looking around for the source of the voice, peering behind roots and ferns for a clue. Finding nothing, she returned to where she'd originally stopped running, deciding that if the speaker could see her from there, then she should be able to see him. Sure enough, she noticed a dancing light next to a paper tree stump, and walked slowly over to it.

It was a Candle, standing six feet tall with arms carved into the slender wax body. The wick formed its neck, and a face was within the flame, brilliant white eyes fixed on her intensely.

Alice smiled, not wanting to upset it any more than she already had. "Pleased to meet you."

"No you're not," the Candle said shortly. "You didn't even know I was here until just now."

"I'm still pleased to have some company," she insisted, gazing up at it.

"You shouldn't be. I'll eat you!"

Alice's heart skipped a beat in alarm. "You'll what?"

"He eats everything, he does," said a Tiger-lily who was growing nearby. "He'd eat me and you and the trees and rocks if he had the chance! He's so greedy, he even eats himself!"

"It's true," the Candle nodded, his voice tightening. "Why do you think I'm here, all alone? Nobody will dare come near me, in case I eat them, but I simply can't help myself." He swallowed hard so he couldn't sob. "Anyway, what's your business here, girl?"

"Nothing, really. I need to get to the studio," replied Alice.

"How do you suppose you'll do that?" asked the Tiger-lily.

"Well, I'll just go back the way I came."

"Impossible. You've already come that way. You can't take the same steps twice. Just like you can't have yesterday be today, or tomorrow, or vice-versa and versa-vice!"

Alice threw up her arms in frustration. The Rabbit had said something similar, but *he* was the one who'd brought her on this little walk in the first place.

"So what should I do?" she snapped to nobody in particular. "Do I have to keep on going forward forever?"

"Why, certainly. Everyone has to, don't they?" The Candle's flaming head bobbed slightly. "If they have legs or wheels, of course, unlike me. So I go downwards instead."

Alice thought for a moment. "I don't know... in the book, the Hatter said that time had stopped on the tea party, so that wasn't always going forward, was it? *That* was stuck."

The Candle made a humming noise. "But if you get stuck, then you'll never go forward – or backwards, or upwards, downwards, diagonally... you'll just be frozen as you are now. Would you be able to blink, or breathe, I wonder? I don't know... maybe you'd find out why a writing desk is like a raven, anyway."

"She should see the Rat King!" the Tiger-lily piped up excitedly. "*He* does everything backwards, he does! He'll be able to tell her how to get back, surely!"

"The Rat King?" Alice repeated, not sure what to make of a name like that. "Where would I find him?"

"The where hardly matters, don't you understand that yet?" replied the Candle. "To you, he is forward: you must put one foot in front of the other to get to him."

"I'm not sure I do understand," said Alice, "but I'll take your word for it."

"Take more than his word!" the Tiger-lily cried. "Take *him* with you! I'm tired of always watching him in case he tries to eat my petals!"

"A mere mouthful, you'd make!" the Candle snapped. "Hardly worth the effort!"

"Don't argue, please!" Alice said sternly; then she looked over the Candle. "I'm afraid I can't take you with me. You're even taller than me; I can't carry you."

"Then give him some of that!" the Tiger-lily nodded her head at the scraps of paper mache that were still clinging to Alice's skirt. "That will do the trick! Mushrooms always do!"

Alice frowned, gathering a few of the pieces in her hand. "This isn't mushroom. I don't think anyone could eat this."

"Try it," the Candle hummed, looking at the paper like a starving man at a feast. "Oh, let me try it!"

"Well... I suppose it can't hurt," Alice said, and carefully tossed the paper towards him.

The Candle expertly caught them all in his mouth, and they ignited, turning to flame and ash as soon as he touched them. He swallowed them; then his body began to shrink, his head flickering as it followed. Before long, he was the size of a normal candle, and instantly began eyeing the Tiger-lily.

"You're bigger than me now, much more than a mouthful!" he laughed.

"Don't you dare!" Alice cried, snatching him up before he could lean too close to the flower. "Isn't it enough that I already gave you something to eat?"

The Candle grumbled. "Alright, fine."

"See? It was mushroom, wasn't it?" the Tiger-lily said triumphantly in the middle of tidying her petals. "You should listen when people tell you things, girl. They probably know more about it than you do, and I knew what that was all along!"

Alice went to argue, but then she remembered where the pieces of paper mache had come from: her falling into the fake mushroom on set. And what was it the Caterpillar said in the story? *One side will make you grow taller, and the other side will make you grow shorter.*

She bid the Tiger-lily goodbye, and started to walk into the forest, the Candle clutched in her hand. She decided it didn't really matter which way she went, but chose not to follow the Rabbit, because then she'd likely find herself at his house. And after the way he'd run off, she didn't like the idea of actually getting stuck inside it.

The Candle lit the way well, revealing more and more pop-up trees and shrubs. The darkness closed in around them, but Alice wasn't fazed by it now she had a companion, even if he was greedy and short-tempered. But, she supposed, most people were in Wonderland, and that had to be where she was. Why else would the White Rabbit have come? And after all, she was *an* Alice, playing the part of *the* Alice, so it had to make some kind of sense.

"Why are you walking so fast?" the Candle asked suddenly, cutting her off from her reverie. "Slow down, for goodness sakes! Otherwise my head will blow back and I'll have to take a bite out of your hair!"

Alice hurriedly swept her ringlets over her shoulders so they weren't in reach. "Well, I don't have a lot of time, you see. I can't stay here for too long."

"Well, walking fast won't do the trick," the Candle remarked. "Do you think the world's as slow as you are, that speed will let you beat its spinning? Of course not!"

Alice nodded. "I remember that in the book: the Red Queen had to run very fast to stay in the same place... so does that mean that even if I try to get back quickly, I'll just slow myself down instead?"

"Precisely!" replied the Candle. "But what's this book you keep speaking about? I don't see any book."

"The book that the movie is based on," she said.

"What movie?"

"The one I'm making."

"How can you be making something?" the Candle snapped. "You're not holding anything that would suggest a making! No scissors, no glue, no building blocks… you can't make something without things to do the making!"

"All the things are back in the studio, where I need to get," Alice tried to explain. "But everyone's been saying that I can't get *back* to it, so I'm quite confused."

"Well, everyone is right!" the Candle said. "Time doesn't go *tock-tick*, does it? It goes the other way, so you have to as well. What's so confusing about that?"

Alice fell silent, and quietened the Candle by finding a paper leaf that had fallen off a tree and holding it over his head. His flame leapt with excitement, so strongly that Alice had to drop the leaf before he could burn her fingertips. The Candle caught it with his tongue, like a frog snatching a fly out of the air, and swept it into his mouth.

Alice let him get on with it, continuing her walk through the shadows. When she began to wonder if the forest would ever start to thin out, she noticed the ground felt a little different underfoot. She glanced down, and saw that the grass had disappeared: now there was a solid chequered floor, with the darker squares the same shade of blue as her dress. Where the trees had been were now walls, also blue; creating a long corridor that stretched ahead. There were no doors leading off it, but she saw some openings, and when she looked into them as she passed, she realised they were more corridors.

"Where did this come from?" she mumbled to herself, turning into one of the second passageways. Along the walls in here, however, writing was scrawled from wainscot to ceiling. She held the Candle closer so she could read the words.

All the king's horses and all the king's men
Couldn't put Humpty together again…

She suddenly heard a loud squawking noise coming from down the corridor. Not waiting for anxiety to get the better of her, she ran onwards, dodging an assortment of toys that were scattered across the floor. The Candle exclaimed in fright at the sudden movement, but Alice ignored him, turning corner after corner without thinking about it. It wasn't as though getting lost in this maze would matter – she was lost enough already.

"Hello?" she called out. Her voice echoed around her in an eerie choir.

"Hello?" said a new voice behind her. Alice looked around, and noticed a brightly-coloured bird standing in one of the nearby hallways. Upon closer inspection, she recognised it as the Lory, but it was a real one this time, not the costume which Bill had been wearing during the last scene.

She approached slowly, not wanting to alarm it. "Nice to meet you."

"You've only just met me," said the Lory, "so how can you tell whether it's nice or not? We may not get along at all, young lady."

"I'd like to think we would, though," Alice insisted.

"Thinking is not equal to knowing," the Lory declared with an air of pompousness, "and I am older than you, so I must know better."

"How old are you?"

"What does it matter? I am older than you, and that is all."

Alice couldn't bring herself to press the bird, because she remembered reading somewhere that Lories could live for about twenty years, and that was almost twice her age now. So she shrugged it off and decided to change the subject.

"If you know more, could you please tell me how I could find the Rat King?" she asked.

The Lory tilted its head to one side in a very parrot-like fashion; then fluffed its vibrant wings. "I certainly could."

"Then would you?"

"Oh, those feathers look delicious!" the Candle suddenly started to murmur. "Oh, let me… just one feather…"

"Absolutely not!" Alice snapped, but the Lory had heard him, and sprung back in panic.

"Keep that thing away!" it cried.

"I am!" Alice said, and she gave the Candle a sharp flick with her finger. "Stop it right now! You can't still be hungry! Now behave yourself or I'll blow you out!"

"Weren't you listening? I'm always hungry!" replied the Candle, spitting a spark at her. "Give me a feather!"

Alice rolled her eyes, unwilling to listen to him any longer. So she drew in a breath and then puffed it straight at him. The Candle's mouth opened a little in faint surprise; then his entire head burst out, leaving nothing but a thin trail of smoke twirling upwards from his neck.

"Thank you," said the Lory, instantly more relaxed. "Oh, don't worry about him. He's just sleeping. Put a match to him and he'll be awake and eating more than ever."

Alice placed the Candle on the floor, making sure to stand him upright so no wax would leak over the tiles. Then she kicked a few dolls out of the way so they couldn't ignite him if he accidentally tipped over.

"Now will you tell me how to reach the Rat King?" she asked, lacing her fingers together in front of her. "It's important that I speak with him, you see."

The Lory huffed impatiently. "How am I supposed to see something like that? I can see you, and I can see the walls, and the words on them, but how can anyone see what you speak? You're a strange creature, girl!"

"It makes sense where I come from," Alice replied, becoming defensive. "Why can't anybody just understand what I'm saying? It's not that hard!"

"Well, there's your problem," said the Lory. "Words aren't hard or soft. They're simply words. You make too much out of something that really doesn't need it."

"*I* make too much of something?" Alice could barely believe her ears. "I could beg to differ, but I honestly don't want to get into another endless conversation like this. Come, tell me how I can get to the Rat King."

"Follow the ticking," the Lory chuckled, as though it were the most obvious answer in the world. "Do you hear it?"

Alice shook her head. "No. But I'm sure that if I keep walking forwards, I'll have to find it sooner or later."

The Lory nodded slowly. "Good. You're smarter than you look, you know," it said. "But I am older than you, so I know much more – remember that!"

Alice didn't reply, and instead began a new journey down the nearest corridor. All the time, she listened hard, but didn't hear anything except the occasional squawking from the Lory behind her. She started counting how many toy cats she could see among the mess on the floor, but she lost track at around twenty-three, so she turned her attention to the words on the walls. They looked as though they were all from poems, which she vaguely recognised, but she was moving so fast that she only caught a line from each one.

> *For he can thoroughly enjoy the pepper when he pleases...*
> *But I was thinking of a plan to dye one's whiskers green...*
> *The further off from England the nearer is to France...*
> *Eager eye and willing ear, pleased a simple tale to hear...*

The metronome started to tick.

Alice would have recognised it anywhere: a deeper sound than what she knew came from a watch. It brought a burning picture to her mind: the instrument sitting beside the camera to help guide the pace of filming as the lever was turned.

There could be no doubt: that was what the Lory had meant. Desperate not to lose it, she hurriedly began to follow the noise, trying to ignore how monotonous the maze of corridors seemed. She supposed that sight wasn't the best sense to rely on in this place: the poems were all fractured, and she could have spent the rest of her life running back and forth down the passageways trying to find the next line in any one of them. The rhymes seemed to be singing at her, trying to work their way into her ears, but she paid them no attention, not letting her concentration break.

After what seemed like forever, she finally turned a corner and found the metronome. It was giant: at least twice her height, with its pendulum swaying idly, only just stopping short of hitting the walls. But behind that, where the line of numbers should have been, there was nothing but a gaping black hole.

Alice studied it for a moment. No light managed to flow into it; she could feel its pull on her body like a compass needle turning to north.

"I wish I had that annoying Candle with me now," she muttered. "It looks as though this is the only way I can go."

The metronome carried on ticking, beckoning her closer. She swallowed nervously; then walked forward before she could think about it too much, using the pendulum to haul herself up onto the base. The swaying movement disorientated her and she almost fell off, but she grabbed hold of the instrument's frame, and stepped into the abyss.

To her shock, she didn't fall. Instead, the darkness opened like a door, and she carried on, hands in nervous fists as she went. A blast of bright light exploded ahead, dazzling after the gloom of the forest and labyrinth, and she covered her eyes.

"Child, here look! Them meet you when somebody at look to not you of rude very it's!"

The voice was so severe that Alice immediately lowered her hands. Still squinting, she glanced around, trying to figure out where she was now.

Surrounding her was a majestic hall, with huge pillars arching towards a ceiling so high that she had to crane her neck to see it. There were windows on every wall, letting in the blinding light, and the floor was carpeted with an array of living flowers, all whispering amongst themselves. At the far side of the room, directly opposite, was a figure about the same size as her, whom she supposed had been the one who'd spoken.

She smoothed her skirt and walked closer, being careful where she placed her feet so she wouldn't step on the blossoms. As she drew near to the figure, her eyes adjusted, and she saw him properly for the first time.

It was the Rat King. He was perched regally on a throne, thin face turned upwards, whiskers occasionally twitching as he sniffed. But then Alice noticed he wasn't the only rat there. At least five others were underneath him, forming different parts of his throne. Two of them were the armrests on which he laid his front paws; another was perched on the floor to act as a tuffet. But when Alice looked closely, she saw that all the rats were joined together, their tails knotted in an intricate yet haphazard way, and it was this which made the cushion on which the King sat.

The sight was alarming, but Alice quickly remembered her manners and curtsied. "I'm so sorry."

"Are you course of!" the Rat King snapped. "Alice isn't it if, now. It isn't, right that's?"

Alice frowned, trying to follow the conversation. It was very perplexing to hear every word spoken backwards, but she supposed she was grateful that he wasn't pronouncing them backwards too.

"Yes, Sir," she replied eventually. "I was told to come to ask you about getting to the studio."

"Now you were? Days these people! To have they way the except anywhere go to wanting always!" huffed the Rat King. "Me see and come to you told who?"

"The Tiger-lily," she replied.

"Trouble causing sisters your of one!" the King barked at the live flowers, but none of them stopped to listen, so he carried on talking to Alice. "Assistance of be can I suppose I. Backwards go to want you so?"

"Yes, I do."

"There over go then."

He pointed behind Alice. She turned around, and was surprised to find that the metronome door had disappeared. In its place was a large mirror, bound in an ornate frame. But it showed absolutely no reflection, not even of the gossiping pansies directly in front of it.

"What good will that do?" Alice asked.

"Think you do what?" replied the King.

"Isn't the whole point of a looking glass that you can look at what's in the glass? There's nothing in there, or outside it. So what can I do with it?"

"It at look to you tell didn't I!" he said impatiently. "Looking *not* is backwards of point whole the. Them see mustn't you then, steps your retrace to want you if!"

"It's all very confusing!" Alice cried, unable to help herself. "Why does everything have to be so difficult here? And I thought making a movie was hard enough!"

"Complaining with confusion mix don't! Nice taste doesn't it." The Rat King ran a paw through his whiskers. One of his armrest neighbours did the same; then instantly fell asleep. "Back go!"

Alice sighed dramatically. "If it does please you, Sir," she said, too tired to mask her frustration.

She glanced over her shoulder to gauge where the mirror was, before carefully beginning to walk in reverse. She was sure to keep straight in case she missed her target, her eyes firmly locked on the Rat King with every step. Not looking where she was going made her heart beat faster, but she held onto her courage. Backwards was just as unnerving as forwards, and just as unknown, she realised.

She felt her heel tap against the bottom of the frame. She closed her eyes, clasped her hands together, and let herself fall through the mirror.

Coldness clung to her and made goose bumps rise on her arms. She turned over and over, spinning into nothing, humming a little tune to herself to pass the time. It was a good melody for the Lobster Quadrille, she thought, and started to imagine the whiting and the snail gathering on the shingle.

"Alice!" a voice called somewhere in the distance. "Alice, where are you? You'll be late!"

"Late for what?" she mumbled, trying to suppress a yawn.

She opened her eyes. Countless movie props lay around her, highlighted from above as the rainclouds blew away. She was sitting hunched on the stack of doors, a pair of boots in her hands. Across from her, the White Rabbit had disappeared from the rail.

Bill suddenly poked his head around the side of a giant domino.

"There you are!" he exclaimed. "Why didn't you come for dinner? Don't tell me you fell asleep!"

"I… think I did," Alice said slowly. She eased herself off the doors and quickly placed her boots behind a storage crate.

"You lazy thing!" Bill laughed. "Come on!"

Alice complied, tidying her dress and hair before running with him onto the set. The crew members were darting about, some with cake crumbs still on their jackets, setting up the façade of the Rabbit's house. Near the studio doors, another actor was being fitted into the costume; and a woman was busy fixing the smashed mushroom.

Alice glanced at the dais, where Pete the Rat was fussing over a camera. An idea came to her, and she edged closer, raising her voice a little to distract him.

"I had an idea to make the caucus race look strange enough."

Pete cocked an eyebrow. "And what is that?"

She smiled broadly. "Why not run the film *backwards*?"

He went to say something, but paused, staring at her as though he'd never seen her before. Then a huge grin broke over his thin face, and he tapped her cheek with one finger.

"You know something, I think that might actually work! Good thinking, kid!" he said. "Now, to your positions, everybody! Let's get this scene done and then we can all go home!"

The metronome started to tick again.

THE HARBINGERS

T he first thing Clementine heard was the sound of Imogene crying. She rolled her eyes, trying not to listen. Wailing was unavoidable with a baby, but why did they always have to make a noise like *that?* It was as though her mother was raising a banshee, not a human being.

Composing herself, Clementine smoothed her skirt and picked up her doll. She caressed the smooth porcelain face, staring at its glass eyes. Then she braced herself, and walked into the adjoining room.

Her mother was sitting on a low stool near the fireplace, bouncing the screeching infant on her lap. Its chubby face was reddened with agitation, mouth wide open to expose toothless gums.

Clementine hid her disgust, letting a mask of sweetness fall across her face.

"She doesn't sound happy," she said.

Her mother nodded with an exhausted smile. "She'll calm down soon enough. Where are you going?"

"I thought I'd go pick some berries," said Clementine, grabbing a basket off the sideboard. "They should be ready today."

"Oh, you dear thing," replied her mother. "That would be wonderful."

Clementine approached and hugged her warmly, before turning her attention to the baby. She tapped it on the nose with one finger.

"Now, you behave yourself," she scolded. "If you do, you'll grow up quickly, and then we can play all day long. You'd like that, wouldn't you?"

Imogene only cried louder. Clementine's eyes narrowed in revulsion, but she quickly pulled it under control. Her gaze fleeted over the locket around the little girl's neck, identical to the one she herself wore, save for the engraved initial on the front. Absently, Clementine's hand crept to her own pendent, tracing the *C* with her thumb.

"I'll go now," she announced, giving her mother a kiss on the cheek.

"Alright, honey. Be careful."

"I will, Mama."

She skipped to the front door, doll held in her elbow, and paused on the steps to pull it closed behind her. As she did, she heard her mother muttering to Imogene.

"She's such a sweet girl, your big sister. One day, you'll be just like her: the kindest child on Earth."

Clementine smirked; then let the latch drop.

She walked slowly along the path, and the great forest towered above her. The trees stretched so tall that she sometimes thought they were holding up the sky, preventing it from crashing onto their little isolated house. It felt as though it had come straight from the pages of a fairy tale, caught between the familiar and unknown.

But she'd learned long ago not to be frightened. There were no wolves or witches like in the stories she'd been told. This was her playground; her garden. With only the plants and birds to see, she could throw away her façade, and expose her true smile to the world.

It didn't take her long to reach the blackberry bush. As she walked over to it, she snatched out at a nearby fern, yanking it clean out of the ground. She swung it around idly for a few moments; then discarded it.

Hands free, she turned to the berries, plucking them from the stems and tossing them into her mouth. She dropped a small handful into the basket. It didn't matter. She would just tell her mother that the crows had eaten the rest.

And her mother would believe her. She'd believe anything, so long as Clementine smiled in just the right way.

Belly full, she skipped off the path, swiping at wildflowers as she passed them. The delicate heads flew in all directions like confetti.

She was decapitating them, Clementine thought. Her hand was a guillotine, and like in the accounts from France, it came down on the necks of traitors. She wasn't sure what the crime was yet; she would think of a reason later.

"I am the queen of my forest," she declared. "And my subjects have displeased me! You will all suffer for it, because that's my law!"

The ground softened underfoot; dirty puddles welled around her boots as she walked further.

She suddenly heard a weak cooing sound coming from behind a tussock. Curiosity getting the better of her, she followed it, and found a dove lying on the ground. It was prostrate, wings splayed, and its chest swollen alarmingly. Clementine supposed it must have been ravaged by a wildcat or fox.

She regarded it for a long moment, her head tilting to the side. She adjusted her grip on her doll, so it hung loosely from her hand by the leg.

"Poor birdie," she said quietly. "You look like you're hurting."

The dove trembled, too weak to do anything more.

"I know what will make you feel better," smiled Clementine, a gleam coming into her eyes. "Don't worry. I'll take care of you."

She raised her arm and threw the doll as hard as she could. Its porcelain face smashed onto the dove, and the white wings stopped twitching.

Clementine chuckled to herself; then strolled away.

It was only a few moments later that her scream echoed through the trees.

Imogene sometimes imagined she heard the cry when she was out in the forest. She told herself it was just the wind, whistling through the branches in a certain way. That was what she'd always thought, having such a rational mind. In a place as endless as this, with no neighbours, and at a few miles' walk to town, it was easy to perceive things that weren't really there.

Her mother believed a different story though. She'd often say, with a faraway pain in her eyes, that it was the last sound Clementine had uttered before she fell into the bog, ten years ago.

All her life, Imogene had respected her mother's wishes and stayed close to the house. If she ever went deeper into the woods, she always kept to the paths, and stayed well clear of the marshy area. It was restrictive and frustrating, but she knew why she had to do it. Her older sister had been her age when she'd set out to pick berries and never come home.

There was no need for tales of monsters and evil beings in a place like this. Reality could bring more horror than any fiction. Her mother's mind was sure proof of that.

Imogene quickly cleared her thoughts and packed some more wood into her pack. She had been sent out that afternoon to collect fuel for the fire. They had more than enough, but the nights were beginning to draw in, and before long winter would be upon them. Preparation and stockpiling were always essential at this time of year.

When she couldn't carry any more, she headed back to the house. It was a single-storey cabin, surrounded by a picket fence that separated it from the sprawling forest outside. She walked to the side wall, where the firewood had been stacked. Emptying her load onto it, she went to find some more, when she noticed a shuddering movement behind the pile.

Frowning, she glanced around it, and gasped. An injured crow was lying there, its head on the ground.

Imogene instantly bent down and gathered it in her hands. It didn't fight her; too exhausted to even try. She checked it over, thinking its wing might be broken, but couldn't find anything that seemed life-threatening. Upon pressing her fingers to its chest however, she found its crop empty.

"You must be hungry," she said in a gentle voice. "Don't worry, I'll give you something to eat."

Cradling the crow close to her chest, she hurried through the front door, heading directly to the sideboard. She pulled a blanket out of a drawer, wrapped the bird in it, and placed the animal in a small wooden box.

"What are you up to, Clementine?" her mother asked, approaching from the other room.

Imogene grimaced inwardly, too used to this by now. "Mama, I'm not Clementine. Remember?"

Her mother waved her hand through the air as though brushing the comment away. "What have you got there? A bird?"

"Yes. I found her in the garden."

"How do you know it's a girl?"

"I don't *know*. I just think so."

Her mother glanced inside at the crow. For a long moment, she didn't react; then walked slowly to her stool in front of the fireplace. She jabbed at the embers with a poker, and red sparks flew up the chimney.

Imogene ignored everything, fetching a small bag of seed from a cupboard. She carefully held the bird between her knees, still cocooned in the blanket, and prised open its beak so she could tip the food down its throat. The crow resisted at first, but then seemed to realise what she was doing, because it sat still and allowed her to continue. Before long, its crop was engorged, and Imogene placed it back in the box with a saucer of water.

"You're not keeping it, are you?" her mother asked tightly.

"Only for tonight," replied Imogene. "I'll let her go tomorrow. I want to make sure she'll be alright."

"Well, don't spend too much time with it. Crows are intelligent things. If it gets too used to your face, it will never leave you alone."

"Yes, Mama."

Her mother paused, looking at her deeply. Then she held out a hand, beckoning her closer. Imogene complied, coming to sit on the floor at her feet, preparing herself for the conversation which she knew was due. A wistful expression flowed into the older woman's eyes as she stroked her daughter's chin.

"You have so much of Clementine in you, you know," she muttered. "How I wish you could have known her. She loved you so much. She always said how she couldn't wait until you were older, so she could play with you properly."

Imogene gave a small smile, toying with the locket around her neck. "Do I look like her?"

"Oh, yes," said her mother. "You have the same little button nose; same blonde hair – you know I can't help dressing it up the same way I always did with hers. You are exactly the same height and build as she was. Especially now you're ten, just as she was. Just as she'll always be."

Imogene nodded, knowing what she had to ask next. "And am I *like* her?"

"She was more imaginative, I'd say. But yes. She loved animals, and the forest, and her family. She adored everything; she was so gentle and kind. You are a spitting image. Sometimes I confuse you, if I see you in the middle of the night – I have to remind myself that you're *not* Clementine."

It wasn't just during the night. Through her whole life, Imogene suspected she had been called by her sister's name more often than her own.

She averted her eyes, trying not to show how much that simple observation could upset her. She knew her mother couldn't help it; the loss of Clementine had shaken her so terribly that she hadn't allowed a single thing to change. A drawing of the first girl took pride of place atop the mantel; her toys remained on the table, never played with, but carefully preserved. Even her bed was still there, with the same blankets on it, in the corner of the room she'd shared with Imogene.

Even this house, tiny and isolated, became a shrine in which her mother lived for Clementine's memory. Despite how near it was to the girl's unmarked grave, the family had never left for town. Imogene had numbly accepted the reason long ago: it was better to stay close for a dead daughter than go away for a living one. All she had to do to keep the peace was wear Clementine's dresses and tie her ribbons into her own braids. It kept her mother contented, and that was all that mattered.

"It's very cold," her mother muttered. "Put another log on the fire, dear."

Imogene did as she was told, lodging it right at the back of the hearth. She received no further reaction; her mother was staring into the distance at something only she could see.

Repressing a lament, Imogene tried another tack.

"Mama? You don't like crows, do you?"

"No."

"Why not? They're only birds."

Her mother shook her head. "Sweetheart, some animals are more than that. They are omens; harbingers of something. A dove brings peace and prosperity. A crow doesn't. A crow brings death."

Imogene frowned. "Not that little one, though. She's nice. She was only hungry." She paused. "Didn't Clementine ever bring crows home when she found them?"

"No!" her mother suddenly shrieked, eyes rolling. "It was a flock of crows that went up in the air, screaming like devils, when she fell into that bog! You keep that thing away from me and get it out of this house!"

Imogene threw her hands out as though to calm a terrified animal. "Mama, don't panic! Everything is alright. I'll keep the crow away. It won't hurt Clementine."

That broke through to her mother, and she slowly began to relax, her breathing becoming more normal. She held a hand to her forehead as though pained.

"Just be sure to release it first thing in the morning," she said. "Promise me."

"Alright. I promise."

"Good girl. Good, sweet girl, Clementine."

Deciding to leave her poor mother to her wanderings, Imogene grasped the box and took it into her room. A tower of her sister's toys loomed over her; countless embroidery samples bearing her signature cursive *C* were framed on the wall. She passed the ghostly bed, deliberately not looking at it, and sat on her own, shadowed in the far corner. She placed the crow beside her nightstand, reached inside, and gently tickled its neck.

"I'll bet you feel better now, don't you?" she asked in a soft voice. "I should think so – that was our very best seed! But you'll be off home tomorrow. That will make you ten times better!"

The crow blinked at her; bent and tried to preen its wings through the blanket. Imogene chuckled, moving the fabric away a little so it could reach. Then a frown spread over her face as she noticed something white amid the black feathers. She pulled it free, examining it in the light.

It was a tiny shard of porcelain, edged with a red stain. Imogene shrugged, deciding it must be berry juice.

The next morning, Imogene woke early. Dawn had swept the overcast sky with a strange directionless light, throwing half-shadows across every surface. There was a chill in the air, and her breath misted before her face.

Throwing a shawl around her shoulders so she wouldn't catch a chill, she slipped her boots on and crept into the main room. Peering through the other door to find her mother still asleep, she quietly heated some milk over the fire and made herself a bowl of thin porridge. Afterwards, she fetched the crow, giving it one last meal of seed.

"I'll be sad to see you go," she whispered to it. "It's always nice to have a new face around here. What with Mama and I always being by ourselves… it does get a bit lonely." She sighed, stroking along its iridescent feathers. "I wish I could have known my sister properly. She sounded so nice."

The crow cawed in reply. Imogene grinned at it; then picked it up, heading towards the front door. She didn't bother leaving a note. Her mother would know where she was, and she'd be home before long.

She followed the path out of the gate and through the trees, gazing at them as she passed. Remembering the warning that the crow wouldn't leave her alone, she supposed releasing it a fair distance from the house would make it less likely to follow her back.

"It's a shame," she said, unable to stop herself talking to it. "I was really starting to like you."

The crow bobbed its head, as though knowing why she had brought it out here. Imogene gazed into its beady black eyes with a saddened smile; then unwrapped it from the blanket and raised her hands. The crow instantly opened its wings and flapped up, coming to rest on a nearby branch. It looked at her, almost expectantly.

Imogene looked straight back.

The crow cawed and soared away. But it flew lazily, and her gaze followed its hypnotic trail through the air.

She mustn't want to leave, either, she thought. *Anyway, there's no harm in following a little, just to be sure everything's alright.*

Nodding to herself, she set off after it, holding up the hem of her skirt so it wouldn't become muddied. Her mother would be so angry if she wrecked Clementine's dress. The blanket slipped from her hand. Gravel crunched under her feet; then fell silent, as she stepped off the path.

The trees seemed taller and thinner than before, like matchsticks. The opaque morning light had descended into a thin mist that hugged the ground like an ethereal lake. The wind lessened, and drifted away to nothing.

On she walked: a white ghost following the little black bird. It often circled back over her head, as though to ensure she was still there. Eventually, it landed next to a bramble bush and pecked at the berries, swallowing them in quick succession.

Imogene watched with a satisfied smile. All her work hadn't been for nothing. She was sure the creature would survive now.

"Well, I suppose I'd better leave you alone," she said. "Goodbye, birdie."

She went to turn and head back the way she had come, but her boots stayed rooted to the spot. Her hair whipped at her face as she looked around. The path was nowhere to be seen. There wasn't even a trail in the dirt which she could follow; the mist had obscured everything below ankle-height.

Imogene's heart began to hammer. Her breathing quickened; a cold sweat broke out on her forehead. The trees seemed to loom over her, like the bars of a surreal cage. The temperature dropped alarmingly and goose bumps rose on her skin.

She spoke aloud to herself, for something to break the silence.

"Don't be frightened. There is nothing in this forest that can hurt me."

The leaves rustled. Imogene frowned. How could they be moving if there was no wind?

Clouds hid the sun, preventing her from using it to find her way. She knew that wandering in a random direction wouldn't be any help, so she forced herself to keep calm, and took stock of her surroundings.

The bramble bush wasn't one she recognised – she usually went left outside the house to pick berries. So she must have turned right instead. But where had she come off the path to begin with?

Something ran behind her.

She shrieked, whirling around so fast that she fell over.

A little figure, about as tall as her, was standing in the distance. Imogene squinted, trying to make it out, but when she blinked, all she saw was another tree, motionless, where the silhouette had been.

The mist flowed away from her, and she looked down without really meaning to. There was a tiny arm protruding from the leaf litter, clad to the wrist in a finely-stitched sleeve. Shifting onto her knees to get better purchase, Imogene grasped it and pulled.

A tattered porcelain doll emerged, its once-neat dress now blackened from seasons of dirt and rain. The scalp was bald in places, with whatever hair left knotted with no hope of being untangled. She turned it over, and yelped with fright. The face was completely smashed, leaving a gaping black hole where eyes and a mouth should have been. And in its place, lodged within the hollow head, was a bird skull, polished white with age.

Imogene staggered to her feet, tossing the doll as far away as she could. She wiped her hands on her skirt roughly, trying to scrub off the memory of even touching it.

"Mama!" she yelled into the empty air.

For a while, nothing happened. Then a voice whispered a response, right beside Imogene's ear.

"Want to play with me now?"

Terror overcame her and she ran. She didn't care which direction she took, so long as it would lead away from here. The crow watched her go, head slightly tilted to one side. It paused to groom itself for a few moments, then took off after her, not bothering to hurry.

Imogene's vision blurred with frightened tears. She wiped them away quickly, choking down a sob before it could slow her. The forest suddenly seemed so much larger than she remembered; her childhood playground now dark and menacing. A strange purgatory fell around her, blocking her off from the rest of the world.

There is nothing to be scared of, she thought viciously. *Nothing can hurt me!*

The toe of her boot hit a clump of earth and she tumbled over. A twig dug into the soft flesh below her knee and her flesh blazed with pain. That only panicked her further, and she threw her head back, screaming.

"*Mama!*"

The crow swooped over her head and dropped something. It bounced off Imogene's shoulder and landed in the soggy grass beside her. Her eyes followed it, and widened as she saw it was a locket.

Her hand flew to her neck to check hers was still there. It was. And then she noticed the front of the new one, elegantly inscribed with a *C*.

She swallowed nervously, looking about, realising with a jolt where she was. Hip-high clumps of reeds and bulrushes protruded from the ground; a pungent damp smell permeated the heavy air. The soil was dark beneath her, compacted and waterlogged.

Somehow, the direction she'd chosen had lead here, to the bog. To the place where Clementine had disappeared.

"Poor birdie," the voice breathed again. "Don't worry. I'll take care of you."

Imogene's heart leapt into her throat. Shaking fiercely, she went to flee. But at the sudden movement, the ground trembled; then gave way underneath her.

She plummeted up to her hips in the loose marshy earth. She tried to pull herself free, only to have the soil suck her in deeper. It dragged at her legs like hidden hands, drawing down with the strength of ten men.

Frantic, Imogene dug her fingers into the bank. The icy water crushed her chest. She gasped for air as the black sludge crept up her neck.

The air exploded with harsh cries as a flock of crows swept through the trees. They came fast and quick, nothing more than dark blurs against the pale clouds. Only the one which Imogene had rescued remained still, watching as they all swarmed together, taking the form of a human child.

The figure approached, staring straight at Imogene. Blonde curls tumbled about her shoulders like a halo, laced with ribbons and a single black feather. A wickedly serene smile traced her lips. She was exactly the same height as Imogene, not having aged a single day.

Imogene whimpered in shock. There was no mistaking her.

"Clementine!" she called. "Help me!"

Clementine shook her head slowly. "I've been waiting to play with you." She smiled wider. "Just like I played with the little dove."

She walked closer, with agonising slowness, and knelt beside the quagmire. For the first time, Imogene noticed that her dress was wringing wet, streaked with dirt. Her hands were bloodied, red streaks stretching to her elbows.

She reached out, gently running her fingers along her sister's jaw. Imogene recoiled at the touch. It was freezing, and damp; the flesh puckered from water.

"You look just like me," Clementine observed. "You've been trying to play *as* me."

"I had to," Imogene gasped. "For Mama!"

The dead girl cocked her head, like a bird. "Do you want me to take care of you?"

Imogene nodded, the movement jarred by fear. The bog drew higher around her chin.

"Get me out," she pleaded, remembering how often her mother had spoken of Clementine's kindness.

"Do you like me?"

"Yes!"

"Are you like me?"

Directly above, the lone crow cawed loudly.

The aimless light began to dim; temperature fell steadily as night drew in. Dried leaves danced their way to earth on a faint breeze.

Imogene traipsed her way through the undergrowth, her body hunched over against the cold and wet. Her dress was almost black with mud, hair plastered to her skin. Her breaths came raggedly; eyes unfocused, staring directly ahead.

As she walked, the forest slowly seemed to remember its old sounds. The branches creaked and moaned when the wind bent them towards each other. Woodpeckers tapped on trunks somewhere in the distance. They all ignored Imogene, and she ignored them. She touched a crowd of wildflowers as she passed them, the edge of her hand sweeping just below the heads.

At last, the shape of the cabin came into view. The windows were aglow with the warmth of candlelight, and a wispy stream of smoke was rising from the chimney. Her heart lifted in relief. Finding new speed, she ran along the path and burst through the door, slamming it shut behind her.

Her mother looked up sharply from the fireplace, eyes widening.

"Goodness!" she breathed, grasping the hearth to steady herself. "What happened to you, sweetheart? Your clothes!"

"I'm sorry I was out so late," Imogene said in a small voice. "I got lost. I fell in the bog."

Tears flowed down her mother's cheeks. Letting out a whimper, she grabbed Imogene and pulled her into a fiercely tight hug.

"Oh, my darling!" she mumbled into her hair. "I thought I'd never see you again!"

Now in the grip of safety, the scope of the ordeal overcame Imogene like a flood. She began crying too, not bothering to stop herself or explain what had happened. All she knew was that she would never step foot off the path again.

"I'm so happy you're home." Her mother kissed her on the head. "Now, go and change before you catch your death, Clementine!"

She rolled her eyes. "Mama, it's me. Imogene."

Her mother chuckled. "Who's Imogene, honey? One of your bird friends? Is she a new *subject* in your kingdom?"

Imogene backed away in horror. Her heart began to pound, and she flung a hand to her chest, knocking against the locket. She glanced at it, and froze.

It was etched with a *C*.

She suddenly felt the muscles in her face contracting, drawing her lips into an involuntary smile.

"Yes, Mama," the other voice said through her mouth. "She's just a poor little birdie I took care of."

Giggling to herself, she skipped away, through the side door. Her mother watched her go, eyes alight with happiness.

"My sweet girl," she whispered. "Sweet, beautiful child."

Hearing her, Clementine smirked as she turned the key in the lock.

She went straight to the preserved half of the room, pulling a clean dress from the chest. As she smoothed it down, ready to put on, she looked out of the window. A dove was sitting atop the woodpile, a black feather near its feet. It stared at her, an almost earnest expression in its eyes, as though knowing it was already forgotten.

Clementine pointedly ignored it, and glanced over her shoulder at the other bed.

"You've stopped crying at last, Imogene," she grinned, her words laced with spite. "Just the way you should have."

Deep in the forest, the lone crow dropped an abandoned locket, reading *I*, into the marsh. It hung on the surface for a fleeting moment, and then it was gone.

DECIDUOUS

The Rackhams. Their very name turned Jacob's stomach as the car trundled along the potholed track. It was a single stretch of gravel, hardly worthy of being called a road, and he'd been following it for the past half hour, working his way through fields and occasional patches of woodland.

It was the only route to Caslowe.

A tyre hit a particularly large bump and Jacob winced. He was grimly thankful it was autumn. Trying to drive on this spine-breaker of a path in the ice would be a death wish.

"Almost there, sweetheart," Martha whispered inside his head. "Almost there."

Jacob fished around in his pocket for his hip flask. He unscrewed it, stuck the rim between his teeth, and took a deep swig before turning his attention back to the road.

The pale sun dipped lower, and the smudge of a village finally appeared on the horizon. It was fenced in on two sides by large gatherings of trees, and on another by a huge salt marsh, extending further than he could see. It was a bleak place, on the edge of the world, hunkering down as best it could in a squatting tumble of streets.

It was small, as he'd been told several times. He guessed there were only around a hundred inhabitants from the looks of things. There was a post office, bakery, church with its drab grey spire stretching as high as it dared. All were shutting for the night.

An elderly woman exited the butcher shop and placed her keys in the door. Jacob quickly stopped the car.

"Excuse me, madam!" he called out. "Could you please tell me where I'd find Mr Walters?"

The woman looked at him for a long moment before pointing further down the road. "End building."

Jacob nodded and carried on. His knuckles went white around the steering wheel. Martha had told him this had always been a tight-knit place, and the war definitely hadn't changed things. The villagers could probably smell a stranger from miles off.

Before long, he looked up to see a sign hanging from an iron bracket. It read: *E. Walters, Solicitor* in fading gold letters. Inside, there was still a gas lamp burning. Jacob drew the car close to the pavement and turned off the engine, knocking firmly on the door. He was greeted by a tall man with a curling moustache, body as thin as a rake.

"Mr Walters?" Jacob asked.

"Yes," the man replied, wrinkling his nose at the smell of alcohol on Jacob's breath. "And you are, sir?"

"I've come to see you about Caslowe Hall."

"Oh, yes. Come in for a moment," said Walters, holding the door wide.

Jacob nodded in thanks and stepped through. He removed his cap and ran a hand through his hair. He knew his appearance wasn't much to applaud anymore, but the least he could do was attempt to make a good impression.

"I won't be able to go over everything tonight," said Walters. "You've arrived a tad later than I expected."

"I had to take a detour some twenty miles back," Jacob explained, tucking his cap under his arm. "They're still clearing up a bomb crater on one of the roads."

"I still don't know why they bothered dropping any around here. There's nothing to hit but cows," muttered Walters, though it seemed more to himself than his guest. Then he cleared his throat and drew a sheet of paper from the topmost drawer in his desk. "So… Jacob Cray, widowed, age thirty-three years, farmer… Eh? And you can afford that vehicle?"

"Martha's inheritance," said Jacob stiffly. "She was left a large sum of money, which subsequently came to me. As I'm sure you know."

Walters gave a small grunt before returning to scanning the document. "So you're here to sort out *another* inheritance, now old Mrs Rackham's popped her clogs," he said. "The Hall was left to your late wife, but the property has now passed to her next of kin. I suppose that's enough for me to hand over the keys."

"Wait a moment." Jacob took a step forward. "You were the one who contacted me about this. I thought I made it clear that I want to sell the Hall."

"Yes, and we'll sort that at a more reasonable hour," said the solicitor. "You're sure you don't want to do anything with it? You'll be hard pressed to find a buyer. I know the War's over, but money's still hard to come by."

"I'm more than certain," replied Jacob hurriedly. "And there's no need to give me the key. I have no intention of going there."

"Then where are you planning on staying tonight?"

"Can you direct me to an inn?"

"Inn?" Walters repeated in bemusement. "Did you see an inn here? What have people got to come and stay around this place for?"

Jacob pursed his lips. After the monotonous journey, he had no more patience to argue.

Walters chuckled softly, bent to reach a lower drawer, and withdrew a large ornate key. He pressed it into Jacob's palm, and Jacob handed over half a shilling in return.

"Well, when can I speak to you about all this?" Jacob asked. "I don't want to be staying any longer than necessary."

"Caslowe's won you over with its charm already?" smirked Walters, extinguishing the lamp. Then he walked to a hat-stand and began pulling on a jacket.

"Well, it's Sunday tomorrow, so how about the day after that? Come at around ten o' clock and we'll sort out this will. There's a telephone at the Hall which I think is still in working order; take my card in case you need to get in contact. And don't worry, I know the number to the place."

"Do you have the will?"

"Safe and sound. I must say though, it's one hell of an odd circumstance."

Jacob glanced at him. The same notion had been running through his own mind ever since he'd left home for this. News of the will appeared out of nowhere, addressed to Martha: the last of the Rackham family before she'd married Jacob. She had been dead for two years, and despite a sizeable sum from her parents, she'd cut ties with them long before that.

But the legacy of Caslowe Hall – the manor house on the very edge of the marsh – had not been left to Martha by either her mother or father. It had come from her younger sister Anna.

But there was one enormous loose end. Anna was also dead. She had passed away a decade ago.

"Now, if you'll excuse me, Mr Cray," said Walters, pulling Jacob forcefully from his thoughts with a polite gesture towards the door.

Taking the hint, Jacob exited and climbed back behind the wheel of his car. Too frustrated to give the solicitor a farewell, he eased the engine into life and followed the road onward, past the last house, and into the fringe of woodland.

The night had drawn in while he'd been speaking with Walters, and though street lamps had been lit throughout the village, here there was no such luxury. Even with the headlights blazing, he could barely see where he was going. The trees wove their branches together overhead like bony fingers, and Jacob shivered, drinking again from his flask.

"Bugger," he snarled when the last drop trickled into his mouth. He shook the flask in futile hope that there was still some left; then slammed it down on the seat beside him.

Eventually, he turned a corner, and found himself before two tall pillars of stone. The gates which had originally stood between them were now trampled on the ground, rusted clean off their hinges. Jacob worked the car carefully over them and trailed the winding driveway. Then the path widened, and the bulk of a huge building loomed against the sky.

Jacob drew to a halt and stepped out, peering up at the house's façade. It was one of the old style: Jacobean, with towering chimney stacks and ornate masonry adorning every wall. The huge black windows were bare of the latticework of tape which had become a common sight everywhere else. Nobody had bothered to protect this place from the Blitz.

Goosebumps rose on his arms. No wonder Martha had run away from here.

"Get inside before you catch cold," she urged; a soft whisper in his ear.

Jacob shook his head hard and pocketed the flask before retrieving his small bag of belongings.

"Not now, darling," he pleaded to the air. "It's hard enough as it is without hearing you here."

"This is my old home, Jacob," Martha's voice said again. "You're bound to hear more here."

"Stop," he repeated, sharper this time. "I love you, but please don't. I can't think too much about what I'm doing."

There was no further sound except the dry rustling of trees swaying in the darkness. Jacob approached the huge wooden door in the porch and slid the key into the lock. At first, it didn't budge, so he rammed it with his shoulder and it finally gave way. A musty smell flew up his nose and he sneezed loudly. Coving his face with a handkerchief, he noticed a small lantern on a nearby table, and took a book of matches from his bag to light the wick inside.

He found himself in a sizeable entrance hall. Paintings adorned the walls, laced with a fine film of silver cobwebs. The fireplace was covered in ash from the last log to have been placed there. Several doors stood out in the walls like crooked brown teeth.

Jacob opened one of them to reveal a kitchen. A range cooker was in the centre under a curving inglenook mantel, and a Welsh dresser stood against the wall, china plates on its shelves dulled with dust.

Thinking quickly, he searched around, and soon discovered another door, which he pulled wide. Sure enough, the sight of a wine room greeted him: a multitude of bottles stacked neatly in a frame of carved wood.

Jacob pulled one free and wiped the label. It was a vintage port, almost as old as he was. Breathing a sigh of relief, he returned to the kitchen, popped the cork, and sipped straight from the bottle.

It was extraordinarily rich and easily the finest drink he'd ever had, but that hardly mattered. He'd lost his sense of taste after Martha died. When the only way to cope had become intoxication, he'd barely cared what he'd put in his mouth so long as alcohol was the main ingredient. And in this forgotten building, he knew he'd need all he could get.

It wasn't just because of his dislike for his deceased in-laws. Caslowe Hall was heavy with the rumours of what had happened ten years ago. Martha's father had been a renowned surgeon, and he'd apparently taken drastic measures to save Anna's life when she fell ill. He had set up a makeshift hospital, right here within the house itself, so he could see to her needs personally. Martha was forbidden from visiting her, even when she breathed her last breath.

And since then, her tomb had never been found.

Jacob stuffed the port into his bag and returned to the hall, raising the lantern higher so he could make out the impressive flight of stairs. He followed them to the first floor, keeping one hand on the thick banister in case a step gave way. Martha's elderly mother had been the last to live here, and even though she'd only died a few months ago, she had kept herself to the south wing and left the rest of the Hall abandoned. There might be damage which he couldn't see.

He made his way along the corridors, searching for a bedroom. He didn't care where; just so long as he could rest his head for the night.

He tried a door at random. The hinges squealed loudly, but Jacob ignored it, and shone the candlelight around the room. It was in the corner of the house, with views of both the marsh and over a section of the garden. But, more importantly, there was an impressive wooden four-poster.

Jacob threw his bag onto it without a second thought, and stole a glance out of the window. The clouds had drawn away now, allowing the harvest moon to pour its ghostly glow across the earth. He saw a small gate in the stone wall which he hadn't noticed before, leading straight onto the marsh. Barely visible through the woody fortress was a folly, standing as a tiny reflection of the manor's grand architecture.

The grounds of the Hall were large and sprawling; several trees had broken free of their previously manicured beds and woven together into a wall of vegetation. The paths were littered with fallen leaves, and classical fountains had run dry; the carved figures perched atop them frozen in a strange stony purgatory.

How often had Martha and Anna run through this garden, laughing, youthful, in the fullness of life? They must have enjoyed the long summer days, feeling the warm season would never end, before the weight of real life came crashing onto their shoulders. Even they had not been immune to illness, sadness, death before their time.

Jacob laid the lantern down and removed his hat and jacket. He flung his scarf over the headboard; unknotted his tie; pulled off his braces until they hung around his legs. He was about to retrieve his toothbrush, when a sudden movement caught his eye.

He stared at the folly, sure he'd imagined it. But there it was again, unmistakable in the moonlight. A human-shaped shadow moved across the window.

Squatters. He might have known there would be some hiding out here.

His temper suddenly boiled. It was frustrating enough that he'd had to come all the way to Caslowe, missed the chance to arrange the sale with Walters, and was now stuck in the godforsaken Hall until Monday. The last thing he wanted was scroungers.

Pulling his jacket back on, he snatched the lantern again and stormed downstairs. He passed through the kitchen to the old servants' wing. A door leading to the grounds lay there, and he drew back the thick bolt. Cool air billowed into his face. He held his jacket shut with one hand and stepped outside, following the path as best he could. Most of it was covered in half-rotten red leaves, obscuring the way into the darkness.

The place seemed more like a wilderness than ever; only small ornaments half-blanketed in limp scrub gave any indication that it had once been a garden. The air smelled of dampness and decay; the soil was spongy underfoot from recent rains. Odd bulges of fungi stuck out from tree stumps like fans, and mushrooms had grown in clumps among the shadows. The once-vivid colours of flowers were now dull and dry.

He fought his way onward, towards the folly, and finally broke free of the clinging vegetation. The little building was surrounded by thin spindly birches, their paper-like bark shining silver in the moonlight. He climbed the flight of steps leading to the door and pushed it open.

He almost fell over in shock.

The entire space was filled with furniture. There was a chest of drawers and a bookcase, covered with ivy tendrils that were snaking down the brickwork. The stained glass window on the opposite wall was broken in several places, providing an entrance for morning glories, their large white petals turning brown at the edges.

Behind the door was a bed, a moth-eaten teddy bear perched on the pillow, next to a sleeping woman. Most of her face was covered by a rosy blanket, but when Jacob raised the lantern to see better, her eyes snapped open.

She flung back the covers and was on her feet in a heartbeat, backing up against the bookcase. Jacob went to hold out a hand to calm her, but instead grabbed hold of the doorframe at what he saw.

She was several years younger than him, with long and limp brown hair that had been combed into something of a respectable style. Her skin was a sickly grey colour; limbs thin and twiggy.

But that was where all normality ended. Twisting shoots protruded from her scalp; drying leaves about her arms. Sections of her skin were covered in what appeared to be mould, forming dark green patches on her neck, legs and shoulder.

Jacob's thoughts flashed back to the bottle of port. How much of it had he drunk?

The woman suddenly darted forward and shoved her way past him, running barefoot into the garden. Snapping to his senses, Jacob gave chase. She seemed to know the wilderness well, because she didn't falter when she reached the wall of trees. But she appeared to be slowing with every step, as though overcome by exhaustion. Before long, her knees buckled and she crashed into a clump of dead ferns.

"No sun..." she wheezed as Jacob arrived. "No sun..."

Jacob knelt beside her, not caring about the dampness seeping up his trousers. He stared at a coating of black fungus on her exposed shoulder blade. She twisted to look at him, eyes roving and unfocused.

"Who are you?" Jacob blurted. "What are you doing here?"

The woman let out a shaky breath.

"Anna," she said; then collapsed back against the soil and didn't move.

Jacob gaped at her. *Anna?*

He slowly reached over and touched the leaves on her wrist. To his shock, they were real, and seemed fused to her flesh. The mould was real too; her skin freezing cold. But it felt deeper than the fact that she was wearing nothing but a nightgown. There was no heat in her body at all. It was hardly surprising she looked so ill.

Barely thinking, he worked his arms underneath her, lifting her off the floor. There was barely a weight to her, as though she were no more than a child. Her head fell backwards limply, mouth opening a little. A putrid smell wafted free with every exhale.

Jacob thought about whether he should return her to the folly, but he was too confused to make sense of his jumble of thoughts. He picked up the lantern as best he could and walked towards the Hall, shutting the door behind him with his foot. He took the woman to the bedroom he'd found and laid her on a chaise lounge beneath the window. When she didn't wake, he stepped away until the backs of his knees hit the mattress.

He sank onto the duvet, still staring at her, and placed the lantern on a table. He had no idea how to process what was going on. Was he seeing things? Even if she had been a squatter in the folly, as he'd originally thought, what was a bookshelf and proper bed doing down there? And how could *vegetation* be growing all over her like a dead tree?

He snatched the bottle and took several huge gulps. There was something wrong here. The entire house felt as though it had eyes, all turned inward on this room, watching for what would happen next.

"Martha?" he said to the air.

"Yes, darling?"

"Your sister *did* die, didn't she?"

There was silence for a long moment. "Yes."

Jacob gritted his teeth as he looked over the sleeping woman. A fat black spider scuttled across her hand; she didn't even flinch.

He knew he wouldn't get a wink of sleep now.

After several long hours of listening to the old house creak and groan all around him, Jacob watched the dawn begin to seep across the sky. He hadn't drawn the curtains, so it filtered softly into the room. Overhead, a tangle of cobwebs swayed to and fro in a breeze he couldn't feel.

The woman was still lying on the chaise lounge. She hadn't moved a muscle all night, and Jacob had kept glancing back to her, to ensure she was really there. More than once, he'd approached and inspected the strange vines, always alarmed to find they weren't fake. But now the darkness was receding, he could see better, and noticed that the leaves were more shrivelled than they'd been before.

The faint sun broke the horizon, and she stirred, instantly inclining her head towards the window. She got to feet and walked past Jacob as though he wasn't there, spreading her arms wide in the thin light. Dust motes floated past her as though suspended in water.

Jacob quietly cleared his throat and she spun around. Several leaves fell off her with the movement.

"Are you alright, Miss?" he asked warily. "Do you feel ill, or anything?"

"I'm fine," she replied.

"Well, you don't look it," he said. "What the hell were you doing in that folly? You're lucky you didn't catch your death. You can't be around here anyway. Who are you?"

"Anna Rackham."

Jacob stopped short. "*What?* Are you serious?"

"Of course."

"How? Anna Rackham is dead. She died ten years ago."

"How do you know?"

"My wife told me," said Jacob. "Anna Rackham left a will that's due to be acted upon. And it's dated 1935; just before she died. She *can't* be alive."

She narrowed her eyes. "Who are you?"

"Jacob Cray," he replied unceremoniously. "Martha Rackham's widowed husband, if it pleases you to know."

Anna's eyes flitted over him, and her brows lowered into a confused frown. "Martha's gone?"

Jacob nodded, but then got to his feet and started to pace the room, braces smacking against his thighs.

"Alright, I've had enough. What the hell is going on? Are you some kind of joker, or what?" He glanced at the bottle of port. "Or was that damn stuff out of date?"

"You enjoy a drink," Anna stated. "Why?"

"Who doesn't?" Jacob snapped. "And what concern is it of yours why I drink?"

"What is it you seek to drown?" asked Anna.

Jacob locked eyes with her. "Look, I don't know what your game is, but you've got to leave. I've got too much to deal with."

Anna cocked her head. "And where do you propose I go?"

"I don't know! Home, wherever that is! Just away from here."

"This *is* my home."

"I don't care how long you've been hiding out in that folly, but you'll have to leave when this place is sold anyway, so why wait?" Jacob walked over and reached out to take her arm. "I'll walk you to the gate, then you be on your way! You can get yourself to the nearest hospital for starters."

"You will not throw me out of my own house!" Anna shrieked, backing away and raising a hand as though to slap him. "Who do you think you are?"

Jacob sighed sharply, but didn't approach her again. "The *late* Anna Rackham wrote a will that left the Hall to her sister Martha. Well, I'm Martha's next of kin, and I'll have nothing to do with this place, do you understand? So you'd better go before I speak with the solicitor."

"I *am* Anna Rackham," she said in a firm voice. "Don't I look like Martha enough to convince you, Mr Cray?"

Jacob bit his tongue and glared at her. But then it struck him just how true her statement was. His wife's hair had been a little lighter, but this girl showcased the same heart-shaped face; green eyes; thin lips. She even had the same lilt to her voice that Martha carried.

"But it's not possible," he insisted. "Even if Anna hadn't died, she'd be in her early thirties by now. You barely look twenty!"

"I've always looked younger than my age," Anna said, with a small smile at the corner of her mouth.

Jacob studied her again; then raised his shoulders in a shrug.

"Alright, I'm just going to go with this," he muttered, grabbing his bag from the end of the bed. He dug around until he found his razor and shaving cream, and strode into the adjoining bathroom.

The sun had risen a little more, so he could easily see his reflection in the old mirror on the wall. His dark hair was bedraggled and shirt creased from being slept in; heavy bruises discolouring the skin below his eyes. Ignoring all that, he set to work lathering the cream over his face. Anna watched in silence for a few minutes before returning to the window.

When he'd finished, Jacob wiped his skin with a sheet of dusty linen from the sideboard; then sat back on the bed and pulled a pack of squashed sandwiches out of his bag. He'd made several before leaving for Caslowe, just in case, and was now relieved he'd thought that far ahead. There definitely wasn't going to be any food in the Hall. He could buy a pasty for the journey home in the village tomorrow.

"You want one?" he asked through a mouthful of dripping. Anna shook her head, still gazing out into the sun.

He tried another tack, curiosity getting the better of him. "Why are you just standing there?"

"I have to," she responded. "I need fresh water, and as much sunlight as I can get. Especially now. It won't be long before winter."

That confused Jacob even more, but he decided not to press her, unsure whether he'd like a more detailed explanation. She was clearly a strange girl, whoever she was, and he sensed he'd have to take today in his stride if tomorrow was going to come any sooner.

He placed the other sandwiches back into his bag and took an apple. Before he could bite into it though, Anna spoke up.

"What happened to Martha?"

Jacob's teeth froze on the skin of the fruit for a moment. Then he lowered it, letting it rest in his lap.

"She was bombed."

Anna looked over her shoulder at him. "Bombed?"

"She'd gone to stay with a friend in the city for a few days, and the planes came over," said Jacob. "A year ago."

"Did she have any children?"

"No. Why else would *I* be the one sitting here?"

Anna pressed her lips together and turned to face him fully. "Why didn't my mother ever hear about it?"

"Because Martha didn't want her to. She never wanted anything to do with the old bat when her parents wouldn't let her see Anna," replied Jacob. "Which brings me to a question I have for you. If you are Anna Rackham, how are you alive? And I want an answer this time."

She looked at him for a long moment, twirling a section of hair around her finger. A small vine became caught in the motion and formed a strange green curl, bouncing when she let it go.

In a single fluid movement, she began walking towards the door. Her bare feet made no sound on the old floorboards.

"Come with me," she said.

Jacob frowned, but nonetheless did as she requested, following onto the landing and towards a second flight of stairs. Yellowed photographs adorned the way, looming in antique frames. He inspected one, of the sisters sitting side by side. Martha was as she had always been, with her bright eyes and broad smile. And as for the girl next to her... there could be no doubt.

Jacob paused, staring at the photograph. Then he looked around at the strange woman, who had paused at the banister, waiting for him. He compared them, and his heart skipped a beat.

It *was* her.

Jacob swallowed. "Oh, God..."

Anna cocked her head to the side like a cat, but didn't say anything. Neither of them moved for a long while, regarding each other. Then she took a single step onto the staircase with an expectant glance. Jacob shook his head sharply and hurried after her, eyes wide as they climbed to the next floor.

"Don't be scared of her," assured Martha, her voice hovering by his ear.

"How is it possible?" he whispered back, as quietly as he could.

"What did you say?" Anna inquired.

"Nothing," Jacob replied, and they carried on to the second floor without another word.

A large chandelier that he hadn't noticed last night hung from the ceiling above the vestibule, strung with as many cobwebs as there were crystals. Some of the plaster had broken off the walls, and more mould had grown in the corners in long murky lines. It was even dustier up here, as though they were entering a part of the Hall which time had truly shut away.

Anna led him further, down a long thin corridor barely lit from windows, until they reached another set of steps. These were more rickety than the grand ones previously climbed, and led to a single dark door near the ceiling. She beckoned Jacob to ascend before her. He did so, wincing as the boards creaked underfoot, and tried the handle.

He was alarmed when a burst of sunlight greeted him through the door. Squinting, he eased his way into the room, exclaiming as several pigeons fluttered past his face. He carefully opened his eyes, and gasped with shock.

He was standing in the attic, its floor invisible beneath a thick covering of leaves. The triangular ceiling was ruptured with a large hole through which the birds flew, exposing beams and tiles from the roof.

There was a desk nearby, littered with papers and the waxy remains of candles; a white coat hung on a hook nearby. At the far end of the room was a shelving unit full of medicine bottles, syringes, and surgical tools. Scalpels and forceps glinted ominously, as sharp as the day they had been made. And against the furthermost wall was a thin bed, enclosed with metal rails.

"Jesus…" Jacob breathed. So this was the infamous 'hospital' to which Dr Rackham had brought Anna.

He moved forwards slowly. There was an uncomfortable chill in the air which set his teeth on edge, especially when he noticed that the bed sheets were spotted with dark stains. He didn't have to guess to know that blood had once been there.

"What happened in here?" Martha's voice trembled.

Anna drifted forwards until she was standing underneath the hole in the roof. She turned her face to it, smiling gently as the sunlight covered her.

Jacob glanced at her before heading to the desk. His hands hovered over the papers, hesitant about disturbing them, so he wove his fingers together and instead read the topmost page.

Wednesday, 15th May, 1935

She is worse today. The corruption has spread and now her liver and kidneys are beginning to suffer. Prognosis from last fortnight's surgery is not promising. I intend to attempt a radical treatment to

prevent the loss of her life. I shall replace the failing organs as needed with outside biological material.

There must be a way for the tissues to heal themselves with only basic requirements – any greater demands on the heart or stomach may shatter her fragile body. At this stage I am willing to try anything to keep her with us. But it is imperative that she is not disturbed or I fear she will not be long for this world.

I will go into the garden tomorrow and select my latest apparatus.

"Only fresh water and sun…" Jacob muttered, remembering what Anna had said in the bedroom.

He turned his eyes to her. She was still standing in the light, arms spread, basking like a flower. The leaves on her arms had turned towards the sky.

Jacob held a hand to his forehead. This was insane. Had her father really done what he was thinking? Had he fused Anna's body with plant life? How was that even possible?

But yet she was still standing there, only a few feet away, when she should be dead.

"What the hell is going on?" he growled to himself. "I've lost it. I've gone round the bend."

"No, you haven't," said Martha.

"But you told me –"

"Who are you talking to?" Anna asked, frowning at him.

Jacob didn't answer, instead scratching the back of his neck agitatedly. He walked closer to her, stopping just short of the hole above.

"Anna... did you *die* in here?"

She made a strange little movement with her mouth, as though attempting to repress a grim smile.

"I'm not dead," she replied eventually, as though it was the most obvious notion. "I'm deciduous."

"What?"

"As the trees grow and sleep with the seasons, so do I. We need the earth and rain to exist; the sun means we always grow. We regenerate, through summer and winter, forever."

Jacob's eyes widened as he fought to keep up with her. "That's why you were in the folly?"

"Father put me there to be closer to nature. Everyone else thought I was in the ground," said Anna lightly.

"But... what about the will?" he asked. "You left Caslowe Hall to Martha..."

"I knew Father would leave the house to me, but he told me I wasn't to see Martha again while I was sick," Anna explained. "I wanted to give her something, in case I didn't get better. I turned twenty-one in that bed; I was of age. I wrote the will stating that when the Hall came to me, it would immediately revert to Martha if I died. Father let me do it; he authenticated it for me, but I suppose it was lost until recently. It must have been found by the family solicitor after Mother died. That wasn't long ago, was it? That's why it's been ten years; why Martha never came back."

Jacob's jaw hung slack and he shook his head in reply. "Why did you never go to Martha? Afterwards, I mean?"

"Well, from what I've gathered from you, she wouldn't have wanted me to," said Anna. "Why did she leave our Mother?"

Jacob twiddled his thumbs. "Because… she was annoyed. She always blamed her parents for keeping her from you."

Anna lowered her gaze miserably. "I never had a chance to apologise to her. But even if she hadn't been forbidden by our parents, *look* at me, Mr Cray." She grasped the folds of her pink nightdress. "What would she have done? I'm not the sister she knew. I'm probably more fragile than when I was ill. It was better this way. Father was right." She sighed. "Better for all of us."

She turned away, approaching the bed. The patch of mould on her shoulder blade had now spread upwards onto her neck, and another section had started to sprout over her left hand. As her movement disturbed the air, Jacob wrinkled his nose at the smell coming off her. It brought to mind the dank coolness of autumn air; of fungi and detritus on the forest floor.

"Winter will be here soon," she said, in the same distant voice she'd used earlier. She angled her body so she was still standing in the puddle of sunlight. "It won't be long before the long sleep."

She trailed her fingers along a bloodstain in the white bed-sheets and sighed deeply. "I wish it could be winter forever."

"Why?"

"Autumn is the season of death. But I remember how the snow covers all that. It makes everything beautiful again."

A wind swept through the hole, bringing with it a shower of fresh leaves and spinning sycamore seed cases. They whirled around, caught in a miniature cyclone. Anna watched them idly, catching one in her hand as it blew close to her face. She looked at it with a hint of melancholy before releasing it, letting it descend to the floor, where it lay motionless among its fellows. Then she walked away, eyes distant, back towards the door, and disappeared down the steps.

Jacob stared after her, unsure what to do. He swallowed nervously and glanced around the room again. It seemed like a lost pocket of time, deliberately and perfectly preserved in memory of the youngest Rackham daughter. Even the gaping ceiling seemed fitting, letting in the outside world.

He glanced again at the papers on the desk. A single leaf had come to rest on the one he'd read: a lone red stain against the white.

A chill snapped through his bones, and he hurried away, shutting the door sharply behind him.

When he reached the bottom of the staircase, he caught a fleeting glimpse of Anna's nightdress as she rounded the corner at the end of the corridor. He followed, staying a few steps behind. She returned to the ground floor, keeping the same slow pace, through the kitchen and servants' wing, into the garden. She paused beside one of the fountains, a hand resting on its carved rim, and closed her eyes.

Jacob leant against the doorframe and slowly slid down to a crouch. There was an icy pressure in the air, working deep, engulfing the entire Hall in a strange gloom. Outside, the half-naked trees stood against a granite sky, washed with the drab white light of morning,

After what seemed like an age, Anna still hadn't moved. It was though she had turned to stone, and only the faint waving of her hair in the wind gave any indication that she was real.

Unable to bear looking at her anymore, Jacob averted his eyes and held a hand to his mouth. How was he supposed to process this information?

Rationality still ate at his mind – Anna *was* dead. The Rackham line was gone. That was why Caslowe Hall had come to him, after all.

He let out a shaky breath. "Martha?"

There was no answer at first, but then he felt her: thin ethereal fingers overlaying his own.

"I'm so sorry," he whispered, voice almost breaking. "Did you know about this?"

"No," came the reply. "How could I know? I never saw her again."

"You told me she was dead."

"That's what I was told, by my parents. That is all the truth I have known. But she is not on *this* side with me. She never has been. I see it now: she is on *your* side."

Jacob swallowed, trying to hold back tears. "God, I miss you, sweetheart."

"It is not the end," she whispered. "Darling, it will be alright."

"But... what can I do now?"

"Give her eternal winter." There was a faint smile to the invisible words.

Jacob went to reply, when he suddenly noticed Anna looking over her shoulder at him. A leaf worked free from her head and fluttered to the ground.

"You hear her, don't you?" she said softly.

Jacob hesitated for a moment; then relented with a stiff nod. "Every day."

"Can you see her?"

"No. I don't need to."

The corner of Anna's mouth turned up into a small grin; then she wandered off into the labyrinth of scrub. Jacob watched her go before getting to his feet, clutching the wall for support, and returned to the kitchen. The wine room door was still ajar from last night and he purposefully kicked it shut.

A shrill telephone ring suddenly exploded through the entire house. Exclaiming in fright, he ran into the entrance hall and found the machine tucked away under the staircase. He yanked the earpiece off the hook.

"Mr Cray?" a voice on the other end asked.

"Yes, this is he," Jacob replied warily, trying to bring his racing pulse down.

"It's Emmanuel Walters."

Jacob quickly cleared his throat, aware of how close he'd come to crying.

"What can I do for you, sir?"

"Sorry to disturb you, but I just wanted to clarify something for our meeting tomorrow. You mentioned that you wished to sell Caslowe Hall. Would you like me to contact an estate agent on your behalf? He wouldn't be present when we go over the will, of course, but with you saying you didn't intend to stay for long, I thought we could get through everything in one day. Would that be convenient?"

Jacob faltered, mouth opening and closing for a few heartbeats. Indecision flashed through him, and he glanced towards the nearest window at the tangle of weeds. There was no sign of Anna, but the wind had picked up again, and he could hear its eerie moaning through the rafters overhead.

"Mr Cray? Are you still there, sir?"

"Uh… yes," Jacob stammered. "Mr Walters… I think I'd prefer to leave an estate agent out of our business. At least for now. I'm sure I can spare a few more days to sort the affairs."

"Of course," replied Walters, an oddly satisfied cadence to his tone. "Enjoy your Sunday, Mr Cray."

Jacob didn't reply and replaced the earpiece. He rested his head against the staircase support for a moment, taking a few deep breaths; then made his way to the bedroom before he could think too much over the conversation.

The morning slowly dragged its way into afternoon. Shadows of clouds fell across the Hall as the sun arched through the sky. The treetops rustled idly in the wind. A light rain fell, bringing out the smell of autumn all the more.

Jacob returned to the first floor, exploring where he dared to pass the time, and entered the room beside the one he'd stayed in. It was large, with a semi-circular window that faced the marsh, one corner ruptured by vegetation. Spots of black mould had gathered in the corners of the ceiling, and the pink walls were peeling in several places. Tendrils of plants were strewn across the floor, along with seeds and shrivelled berries. The whole place was bare of furniture, though Jacob could clearly make out where it had once stood. The only thing left to suggest anyone had used the room at all was an old jazz poster, tacked to the chimney breast.

He supposed this place must have been Anna's. She'd only been a year younger than Martha, but Jacob knew his wife had always loathed pink.

He thought back on Martha's stories of her late sibling. When she became ill, it had marked the beginning of the Rackham family's fall. After Anna's supposed passing, her parents treated Martha so coldly that she never forgave them. Her father went away to serve in Dunkirk and never came back, leaving Martha alone with her heartbroken mother in the ancient house.

In her bid to escape the stagnation, Martha had found Jacob, but she never lost her resentment from not being allowed to mourn her sister. She'd passed it onto Jacob, and neither of them had ever visited the Hall again. Even when Martha herself died, Jacob had always stayed clear of her ancestral home.

There was just something about this place that kept them away. The memory of Anna had become a strange taint of both love and hate over all who heard her name; all who treaded where she once had.

"Ironic that the plants have come inside," Martha said.

Jacob closed his eyes, knowing instantly why the room was empty. Dr Rackham had moved everything to the folly, taking care that the elder daughter never saw it. But the ivy and creepers had still come searching for Anna here.

He walked to the window; looked over the marsh. The tide was on the turn, exposing a network of thin channels through an uneven horizon of cordgrass. Only hardy things could grow out there, being constantly submerged by the saltwater. No shrubs or trees survived, not even close to land proper.

An idea formed in his mind. He mulled over it, pondering with dire uncertainty.

Why didn't he just finish what he came here for; sell this godforsaken plot, get out of Caslowe forever, and put the money towards his farm? The War had been tough on everybody; just because the battles had ceased didn't mean times weren't still hard.

But that was before. Now, there was something he had to do.

"Go," Martha whispered, sensing his intentions.

Jacob waited until the sun slipped below the murky horizon; then he buttoned his jacket and returned downstairs. He stepped out of the servants' door, moving quickly, letting the moonlight guide him.

The folly appeared through the trees. Sure enough, when he peered inside, he found Anna asleep in her bed; using the hours of darkness to rest like the plants around her.

Jacob drew back the blanket and picked her up, trying not to think too hard on this. She stank of decay, and he had to press his lips together to keep from gagging. He wondered how she might have looked at another time; covered with little blossoms in spring, or clothed in rich greenery at midsummer?

For as gentle as he tried to be, Anna's eyelids fluttered and she looked at him.

"What's going on?" she asked.

"I'm taking you to see Martha," replied Jacob quietly. "Go back to sleep, alright?"

Anna nodded, a contented smile on her lips, and instantly returned to her slumber. Jacob adjusted his grip; descended the folly steps and followed a thin path in the direction of the gate. He lifted the latch and wedged it open with his foot, walking out onto the marsh. It stretched all around them in vast monotony, broken here and there with rough tussocks. The occasional bird rose from the grass when it heard Jacob's footsteps, taking to the air in a swarm of black feathers.

The tide wasn't far away. It would be at the high point before long.

Jacob reached a small mound and softly laid Anna on it. As though sensing her presence, the shoots in the mud inclined towards her, and the tendrils on her body responded in kind.

She stirred a little, still smiling, as though caught in a pleasant dream. But already Jacob could see the salinity working its way into her. Where she touched the damp ground, her bare flesh was wrinkling and bloating.

She didn't react except to mutter, "Hello, Martha," to the wind.

Jacob sighed, taking a few steps away from her. Then he walked back the way he'd come, water splashing up around his trousers, the stars extending over all he saw. When he returned to the gate, he hesitated for long enough to look over his shoulder.

The briny water had risen, and there was nothing left of Anna except a tangle of brown roots.

The next day, Jacob woke early, the emptied bottle cradled in his elbow. He grabbed his watch to check the time, and hurried to the bathroom, running his razor over his stubble as quickly as he dared. Today was Monday; time for his meeting with Walters. Time for him to finally leave Caslowe Hall.

Pulling his braces onto his shoulders in mid-step, he snatched his bag and walked downstairs to the kitchen. He pulled his hip flask from his pocket and opened the wine room door, deciding to refill for the journey home. It didn't matter that he wasn't coming back here; he couldn't be too careful.

He paused, one hand hovering on the handle. Had he drained that entire lot of port last night? How was he not hung over?

Then a horrid suspicion gripped him.

Had he imagined everything? The hospital; the papers; Anna?

His eyes turned to the garden. Not wasting a moment, he ran through the back door and tore his way into the thicket. Before long, he arrived at the folly and burst inside.

All the furniture was gone. The floor was blanketed in old leaves, and the only thing that lay among them was a teddy bear. Jacob picked it up, staring at its faded face. He stepped outside again, glancing in the direction of the gate.

He went to head over there, to check the tussock, when his foot caught something and he tumbled face-first onto the ground. The flask flew from his hand.

"What the hell?" he muttered, starting to tear away at the undergrowth. It hadn't been the web of vines which had tripped him. It felt like something much more solid.

After several inches' worth of digging, he removed the final few leaves, and his mouth fell open. A small square stone was embedded in the soil, elevated slightly.

Here lies

Anna Rackham

6th September 1914 – 25th September 1935

Jacob frowned, eyes beginning to rove between the stone, the gate, and the silver glint of his flask a few feet away.

He thought back to how solid Anna had felt when he carried her. That meant she had to have been real, didn't it? It was true that he'd never *seen* Martha since she died, but he knew *she* was real. Or was this dark house full of more ghosts than he'd realised?

He laid the teddy bear on the grave, and a single red leaf drifted into its moth-eaten lap.

Martha's evanescent arms appeared around him, her lips whispering against his ear.

"The season is over, my darling."

ACKNOWLEDGEMENTS

I owe many people thanks for helping me to bring this little book into the world; first and foremost my amazing family. Mum, Dad and Grand, thank you so much for encouraging me to chase all my crazy dreams and helping me make them come true.

Thanks to my friends who I can't imagine life without, especially Rhian – I will always be so grateful for your incredible support from day one. To all of you, whether I know you physically or via social networking, thank you from the bottom of my heart.

Thank you to all my fellow authors, artists and bloggers who have been there and helped me in too many ways to count. Thank you for your support, reviews, collaborations and hard work: all my friends at Staccato; Melissa and Allana at Girls Heart Books; Serene; Amber; Tammy; Jessica; Becky; Penelope; Derinda; Katie for going above and beyond with the cover reveal; and my 'big sis' across the pond, Jaime. And you. To every single person who has picked up this book or any of my others, I wish there was a word in the English language which could capture how truly grateful I am to you, my amazing readers.

And, since it's a big birthday for one of the greatest classics ever written, I must thank the genius of Charles Lutwidge Dodgson for giving us *Alice*. Here's to another 150 years of madness and magic!

ABOUT THE AUTHOR

E. C. Hibbs is an award-winning author and artist, often found lost in the woods or in her own imagination. Her writing has been featured in the British Fantasy Society Journal, and she has provided artworks in various mediums for clients across the world. She is also a calligrapher and live storyteller, with a penchant for fairytales and legends. She adores nature, fantasy, history, and anything to do with winter. She lives with her family in Cheshire, England.

Learn more and join the Batty Brigade at

www.echibbs.weebly.com

OTHER BOOKS BY E. C. HIBBS

RUN LIKE CLOCKWORK
Vol I: The Ruby Rings
Vol II: The Eternal Heart

THE FOXFIRES TRILOGY
The Winter Spirits
The Mist Children
The Night River

THE TRAGIC SILENCE SERIES
Sepia and Silver
The Libelle Papers
Tragic Silence
Darkest Dreams

Blindsighted Wanderer
The Sailorman's Daughters
Night Journeys: Anthology
The Hollow Hills Tarot Deck

Blood and Scales (anthology co-author)
Dare to Shine (anthology co-author)
Fae Thee Well (anthology co-author)

AS CHARLOTTE E. BURGESS
Into the Woods and Far Away: A Collection of Faery Meditations
Gentle Steps: Meditations for Anxiety and Depression

Printed in Great Britain
by Amazon

12298741R00054